# Macbeth

**Macduff**
A soldier and the
Thane of Fife

**Banquo**
A soldier and friend of
Macbeth's

**Lennox**
Loyal soldier

**Ross**
Loyal soldier

**Duncan**
King of Scotland

**Malcolm**
Duncan's
oldest son

**Macbeth**
A war hero

**Lady Macbeth**
Macbeth's wife

**The witches**
Three sisters who can predict the future

C. A. Plaisted

Illustrated by Yaniv Shimony

QEB Publishing

# A war ends; new battles commence

Act one

A storm was raging across the heath as three witches gathered around the warmth of their bubbling cauldron.

"We need to find Macbeth!" said one.

"Yes—but where?" asked another.

"After the battles are over," announced the third. "That's when we shall meet him!"

The wind lashed their hair, and lightning cracked in the sky as the witches fled.

Scotland was at war. At his battle camp, King Duncan met with his sons, Malcolm and Donalbain, and other officers from the Scottish army. An exhausted captain approached the group.

"Perhaps this weary soldier will have news for us," the king said.

"Macdonald has shown no mercy in his fighting," the injured captain reported.

Macdonald had been the Thane of Cawdor but had turned into a traitor and joined forces with the Norwegian army to invade Scotland. The king shuddered.

"But we stood firm," the captain continued. "And, thanks to Macbeth's bravery, we have defeated our enemy."

"This is excellent news!" exclaimed the king. "Now—go and see the camp doctor about your wounds."

Moments later, Ross, another officer, arrived back at camp.

"Macbeth is on his way back to camp with Officer Banquo," Ross announced.

"Go and meet him," the king commanded. "Congratulate him on his battle honors. After Macdonald has been executed, Macbeth will take his place as the Thane of Cawdor!"

The storm was still raging when the witches gathered.

"Listen!" hissed one. "I can hear the battle drum..."

"Macbeth is coming!" cackled another.

"Hail to the hero Macbeth!" said the third witch, as Macbeth and Banquo came near.

Macbeth gazed in fear at the sisters as they appeared out of the mist.

"You shall be the Thane of Cawdor, sir," said the First witch.

"And then you shall be the king of Scotland!" said the second.

"And Banquo's children will also be kings," cackled the third.

"Who are you?" demanded Macbeth. "And what are you talking about?"

Just as they had appeared out of nowhere, the witches disappeared without answering. Cool mist swirled around Macbeth and Banquo.

"What was that all about?" Macbeth asked. "No idea," said Banquo.

Suddenly, two dark shapes emerged from the mist.

After meeting the witches, Macbeth and Banquo were pleased to see Ross and his fellow officer, Angus.

"The king is delighted to hear the news of your victory," Ross said, shaking Macbeth's hand. "He wants to honor you by naming you the Thane of Cawdor."

Macbeth felt a tingle go down his spine. What was happening? The first of the witches' predictions had just come true!

"But there already is a Thane of Cawdor," Macbeth said.

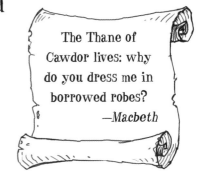

The Thane of Cawdor lives: why do you dress me in borrowed robes?

—Macbeth

Angus shook his head. "Not for much longer. The king is having Macdonald executed for treason."

Macbeth stood silently and then turned to Banquo.

"Perhaps those witches knew what they were talking about," he said quietly. "Maybe your children really will grow up to be kings!"

"Who knows?" Banquo replied. "But I do know I want to get back to camp— come on."

Come what come may, time and the hour runs through the roughest day
—*Macbeth*

This supernatural soliciting cannot be ill, cannot be good
*Macbeth*

After trudging wearily through the mud and rain, Macbeth and Banquo finally arrived back at Duncan's camp.

"Welcome back!" King Duncan said. "We all owe you a great deal of thanks for your courage. You, too, Banquo."

Macbeth shook his head. "I was only doing my duty, sir."

But to show his gratitude, Duncan made Macbeth the Thane of Cawdor, just as Ross and the witches had predicted he would. And in honor of his own son's heroism, Duncan made Malcolm the new prince of Cumberland.

"Now that this war is over," Duncan declared, "I should like to visit you at your home in Inverness, Macbeth. That way we can affirm our friendship."

"My wife and I would be honored," Macbeth said.

"Please excuse me, sir—I must write to her and tell her all my news. She will want to get everything arranged for your visit."

Duncan smiled as he watched Macbeth walk away. Turning to his other officers, he said, "Macbeth is a truly modest and courageous man. We would all do well to follow his example. Come on—let's celebrate our victory!"

Glamis thou art, and Cawdor, and shalt be what thou art promised: yet do I fear thy nature: It is too full o'th'milk of human kindness
—Lady Macbeth

Back in Inverness, in the Scottish Highlands, Lady Macbeth sat alone in her room reading her husband's letter. Thane of Cawdor was a great honor. Now they would finally be rich and powerful! But she also knew that her husband was too kind.

He would let others take advantage of him. As the Thane of Cawdor, he should be exploiting them! Especially if the witches' predictions were to come true. Lady Macbeth had to take control. She  decided to do everything in her power to make sure that Macbeth would become king.

Lady Macbeth read more of her husband's letter. The king himself wanted to visit them! She was just thinking of the parties she could host for the king when she was interrupted. A messenger had arrived at the house.

"The king will be here tonight," he announced.

"Tonight?" Lady Macbeth said. "Then I had better hurry up and get organized!"

Out of the window, Lady Macbeth saw a raven settle on the castle battlements. When she blinked to look at it more closely, this omen of death had vanished...

Lady Macbeth was preparing her home for the king's visit when Macbeth returned. "I am so proud of you," she said. "I always knew that, one day, we would get the power we deserve."

"But I'm not sure the witches were right about me becoming king," Macbeth said.

"The witches wouldn't have said it unless they had seen how great you could be as king!" Lady Macbeth shouted. How typical of her husband to be so pathetic, she thought. "They can see into the future–they know! You have to kill King Duncan. Then you can become king–just as the witches said."

"But does Duncan deserve to be killed so that I can rule?" Macbeth asked. "Perhaps I would be better working alongside him as the Thane of Cawdor..."

"That's enough, Macbeth," his wife persisted. "Who cares about Duncan? Think about what you could achieve if you were king! Listen," she said. "I have it all worked out. We'll ply the king's men with food and drink. And after the king has eaten, he'll fall asleep.

That's when you pounce! You'll kill him, and when his body is discovered, it will look as if his own men killed him in their drunken state..."

Macbeth was worried. "It seems wrong after all the good things Duncan has done for me..."

But screw your courage to the sticking-place and we'll not fail
—*Lady Macbeth*

# Death brings destruction

Act two

Macbeth's mind remained troubled. He wondered if he could really kill Duncan. What if it went wrong? What if Duncan survived? Or someone found out that Macbeth was the murderer?

But Lady Macbeth was insistent that he had to murder the king. Macbeth must become king and then she would be queen...

Macbeth's home was filled with guests that evening. Duncan had arrived with his sons, Malcolm and Donalbain, as well as his personal guards. Banquo also arrived with other comrades from battle, as well as his own sons.

Restrain in me the cursed thoughts that nature gives way to in repose
– Banquo

Lady Macbeth had laid out a lavish feast for her guests. None of them had any idea of their hosts' wicked plan. Every now and then, Lady Macbeth excused herself and slipped off to see Duncan's guards, serving them more and more food and drink.

"You've worked hard for your master," she gushed. "You should share in the treats, too."

And so the charmed guards ate and drank until their bellies and brains were full. They soon fell fast asleep.

Macbeth waited until midnight. By then, his guests had retired to their rooms. Duncan had also gone to his room, unaware that his guards were sleeping next door.

As soon as Duncan's head hit the pillow, he fell asleep. It was a deep, drunken sleep, which meant that he didn't stir when Macbeth entered the room, armed with a dagger in each hand.

While Duncan snored loudly, Macbeth raised his daggers. With one swift movement, the king was dead.

Horrified, Macbeth stumbled into his own bedroom.

"I've done it," he gasped.

"But you've still got the daggers with you!" Lady Macbeth hissed. "You have to take them back to the guards or it won't look as if they did it."

She was calm and focused while Macbeth jumped at the slightest sound.

"I can't face going back," Macbeth said, looking terrified.

"You coward!" Lady Macbeth cried. "Give them to me—I'll do it."

My hands are of your color, but I shame to wear a heart so white
– Lady Macbeth

Alone in his room, Macbeth bitterly regretted his actions. He couldn't get the picture of Duncan's dead body out of his head.

"What's that?" Macbeth jumped as he heard a noise. There was someone knocking at the front door.

"Someone's come!" Macbeth whispered, as his wife came back into the room. "Someone must have found out what I've done. They're here to get me!"

"Don't be ridiculous," Lady Macbeth replied. "Calm down and see who's at the door."

The visitors turned out to be Macduff and Lennox. They wanted to see the king. As Macduff went to the king's chamber, Macbeth continued talking to Lennox, desperately trying to stay calm.

"No!" Macduff's scream rang out. "What's wrong?" Macbeth asked, pretending to have no idea. "The king has been killed!" Macduff wailed. "Wake everyone and bring them here!"

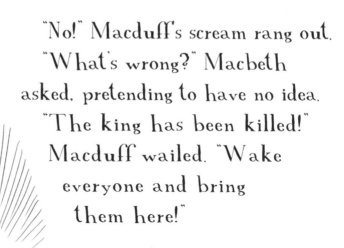

News of the king's death quickly spread to everyone in the castle. Macbeth knew that he had to act fast.

"Where are the guards?" he called, racing into their room. "Look! They're the murderers! The daggers are still in their hands!"

Once more, Macbeth took both daggers in his hands. He stabbed the sleeping guards until they, too, were dead.

By now, Donalbain and Malcolm had been told the news of their father's death.

"I have killed the guards who murdered your father," Macbeth said, as he stood before them, covered in blood.

"What terrible things have happened here!" cried Lady Macbeth, as she came into the room. And, so as to convince the guests of her shock, Macbeth's wife pretended to faint.

O yet I do repent me of my fury, that I did kill them
—Macbeth

"Help her!" Banquo said.

"Come—we must meet to decide what should be done," said Macbeth, as his wife was carried away.

But the king's sons refused to join Macbeth and Banquo. Fearing for their own lives, they fled from the castle.

Macbeth continued to lie as he began to organize the king's burial. Macduff sat with Ross, talking about the horrors that had taken place that night.

> The king's two sons are stol'n away and fled, which puts upon them suspicion of the deed
> —Macduff

"Where have Malcolm and Donalbain gone?" Macduff asked. "And why? Isn't that suspicious? Perhaps they ordered the guards to kill the king."

Ross scratched his chin. "It's certainly strange. And now that the princes are gone, the throne must fall to Macbeth!

He's already shown us his leadership on the battlefield. Now he must be king."

Macduff nodded.

"Come on," he said. "Let's leave Macbeth to his duties. This place is full of horror and sadness. If we stay here too long, we may also fall out and stop being friends. Let's go!"

And after that terrible night, dawn broke on a new Scottish king: Macbeth.

# Power corrupts

## Act three

Lady Macbeth made sure that no time was wasted for her husband to be crowned. Within days, the new king and queen moved into their palace.

One of Macbeth's first visitors was Banquo.

"It seems those witches did know the future!" he said to the king.

Macbeth nodded, remembering that the witches had also said that Banquo's children would be kings one day. "Will you join us for a meal tonight?" Macbeth asked, stifling a yawn. He'd barely slept for the past nights, troubled by guilt.

"I will, sir," Banquo replied. "I have to run an errand but I will be back in time to eat with you."

With Banquo gone, Macbeth began to brood. What if someone wanted him dead, just as he had killed Duncan to become king? Hadn't Banquo just reminded him of what the witches had said? Banquo would surely remember the predictions for his own sons. Tortured by these thoughts, Macbeth convinced himself that Banquo wanted him dead. That must surely be why he was coming back that night—to kill him!

Our fears in Banquo stick deep, and in his royalty of nature reigns that which would be fear'd.
– Macbeth

"I've done all these terrible things, and now they will be done to me, too," Macbeth wailed. "Being in power means that I am vulnerable to attack."

Macbeth decided that he had to protect himself.

Wasting no time,
Macbeth spoke
with one of his most
trusted servants. He
instructed him to
arrange for Banquo and
his sons to be murdered.
Before the night was
over, more blood would
be shed...

Later that night, Lady Macbeth
found her husband pacing up and down in
his chamber. Macbeth was exhausted, but
when he closed his eyes, he remembered
what he had done.

We have scorched
the snake, not
killed it
—Macbeth

"It's all gone wrong!"
Macbeth wailed. "I'm
doomed! Banquo has been
murdered, but his son
Fleance has escaped."
Lady Macbeth gasped.

"You know what this means, don't you?" Macbeth said. "Those witches have been right about everything up to now. It's obvious—Banquo's son will kill me, and he'll become the new king!"

"Stop this!" Lady Macbeth said. "Haven't you arranged a banquet for this evening? All your officers will be coming. It will be a magnificent evening with you as host."

But consumed by guilt, Macbeth continued to brood. No amount of feasting would distract him from what he had done—nor from what the witches had said.

Things bad begun made strong themselves by ill
—Macbeth

As Lennox, Ross, and Macbeth's other lords gathered around their new king's table, they had no idea that Banquo had been killed. Noticing Banquo's empty chair, the guests simply waited for him to arrive.

The only other absent guest was
Macduff. He had kept far away since
Duncan's death.

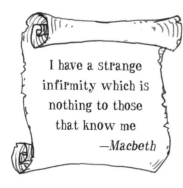

I have a strange
infirmity which is
nothing to those
that know me
—Macbeth

As the guests ate and
chatted, the new queen kept
her guests entertained. But
Macbeth didn't join in the
conversation. He stood up and
went to the window. He looked
out into the darkness and then turned and
stared around the room. Out of the corner
of his eye, Macbeth spotted a shadow.

The misty shape came into view again.
It grew darker as it moved across the room.
Macbeth looked at the others. None of
them seemed to have noticed the shape.
He looked again.

There it was! It had settled in his
chair. The shape got darker and denser. It
gradually formed into the shape of a man.

Macbeth struggled to breathe. He felt
like he was choking.

The shape opened its eyes
and looked back at
him. Sitting in the
king's chair was
Banquo's ghost!
    "Get out of here!"
Macbeth screamed.
"Stay in the ground
where you are buried!"
    Everyone in the room
turned and stared at Macbeth.
Had the king gone crazy?
    "Are you all right?"
Ross asked.
    But Macbeth
didn't hear him.
Instead, he
continued
ranting at a
ghost that
no one else
could see.

"Don't worry," Lady Macbeth announced. "Pay no attention to him. He's fine—he does this quite often. It's an illness he's had since childhood." Knowing that the sleepless nights were driving her husband crazy, she lied to her guests.

Think of this, good peers, but as a thing of custom
—*Lady Macbeth*

But Macbeth's guests were unable to ignore him, despite what their queen said.

"I think we should go," Lennox said. "Perhaps the king will be better in the morning."

Lady Macbeth nodded, looking at her husband with concern. "Good night to you all," she said as they left. But the evil new queen knew that the king would be no better in the morning. He was living his worst nightmare.

"Help me!" Macbeth wept, as he and his wife sat alone. "I fear more blood is going to flow!"

"Shush, husband," Lady Macbeth tried to soothe him. "Where's Macduff? Why didn't he come?"

Blood will
have blood
—Macbeth

"Did you invite him?" Lady Macbeth asked.

"I thought so," Macbeth replied. "Those witches will know where he is! They see what the future holds. I will find them tomorrow and ask for their help!"

Deep in the palace cellar, Lennox met with another one of Macbeth's lords. Unsettled by Macbeth's strange behavior that night, they were worried about their new king.

"I think Macbeth was right to kill Duncan's murderers," Lennox announced.

"But Duncan's sons must be guilty, too, or they wouldn't have fled. What's wrong with Macbeth? He's acting like he's gone crazy!"

The other lord nodded. "I've just had news of Macduff. It seems that he has fled to England to raise an army to attack Macbeth! Perhaps Macbeth won't remain our king for long..."

# Yet more trouble brews

Act four

Under thunderous skies on the heath,
Macbeth found the three witches
hunched over their cauldron. They
were busy mixing their spells when
he appeared.

"He's here!" the first witch announced,
as Macbeth staggered toward them.

"I need to know what's going to
happen next!" Macbeth cried. "You have
to help me!"

The witches cackled.

"We'll summon our magic for you!" the
first witch said, throwing some pigs' blood
into the cauldron. The
witches started mumbling
an incantation.

"Show us!" they all
shrieked at the
bubbling potion.

How now, you
secret, black and
midnight hags!
—Macbeth

34

Double, double, toil
and trouble: fire burn,
and cauldron bubble
—*The Witches*

There was an explosion of smoke, and out of its curling wisps appeared a ghostly head.

"Macbeth, Macbeth, Macbeth: beware Macduff!" it whispered.

Macbeth gasped. So it was true. Macduff wanted to get rid of him!

With a loud roar, flames shot from the cauldron. As sparks rained down, the bloodied ghost of a child appeared before Macbeth and spoke.

"None of woman born shall harm Macbeth!" it said and disappeared.

"So I don't need to fear Macduff after all?" Macbeth said.

He couldn't think of
why Macduff's mother
would not have given
birth to him. But before
he could make sense of
the message,
there was a flash of light
and another ghostly
child appeared.

"Macbeth shall never
be vanquished until Great
Birnam Wood to high Dunsinane Hill
shall come against him!"

Macbeth wept with relief as the last
vision faded from view. "So I am safe!" he
sobbed. "How can woods move and fight
me?" Looking up, he saw a dreadful sight,
"But what is this? Help!"

From all directions, a ghostly army
came toward him. There were nine men, all
bearing crowns of Scotland. And among the
phantoms, Macbeth spotted Banquo.

Macbeth's blood ran cold. "Help me!"
he groaned, turning back to the witches.
He heard only a faint cackle. The witches
had vanished. Whirling around to face the
ghosts, he saw that they, too, had disappeared.

"Sir!"

Macbeth jumped. It was Lennox!

"Did you see those witches? That army
of ghosts?" Macbeth asked.

"No, sir." Lennox shook his head,
increasingly worried about Macbeth's
sanity. "But I bring news of Macduff. He's
fled to England!"

The pair walked back across the heath in silence. Macbeth was deep in thought. If only he had killed Macduff as planned! He cursed himself for having hesitated when he had the perfect chance. Back at the palace, Macbeth ordered his men to murder Lady Macduff and her son immediately.

> The castle of Macduff I will surprise; seize upon Fife; give to the edge of the sword his wife, his babes
> —Macbeth

In England, Duncan's son Malcolm was unaware that yet more murders had taken place in Scotland. He met with Macduff to test his allegiance. Was he loyal to Scotland? Or did he support Macbeth?

"I don't trust Macbeth," Malcolm said. "But I am too weak to be king myself. I am easily led astray."

"That's not true, Malcolm," Macduff said. "You would make an excellent king for Scotland.

> I am not treacherous
> —Macduff

You are brave and committed."

"Yes—but I'm not sure that you are," Malcolm went on. "After all, you've abandoned your wife and child."

"I had no choice," Macduff said. "I had to flee Scotland to get help. And here I am, Malcolm, promising you my support!"

Malcolm looked at his comrade. Could he trust him? Could he trust anyone anymore? But his thoughts were interrupted by a noise outside. The door burst open—it was Ross.

"Macduff!" he gasped. "I have found you! My lord, I'm so sorry but I bring terrible news about your family..."

Macduff screamed in despair when he heard that his entire family had been killed. His grief turned to fury when Ross told him it had been at Macbeth's command.

Wiping tears from his eyes, Macduff turned to Malcolm.

"My revenge is to fight Macbeth," he exclaimed.

"Then we are ready to go to battle," Malcolm said. "Macbeth must be destroyed. Just like he has tried to destroy Scotland!"

Let grief convert to anger
—Malcolm

# Fate catches up with King Macbeth

## Act five

The witches' prophecy had convinced Macbeth that he was invincible. But now Lady Macbeth was terrified. Her dreams were filled with visions of her husband's terrible deeds. She was haunted with guilt at her part in the crimes. Lady Macbeth even imagined that her hands were still covered in the blood of those she had helped murder. No matter how hard her doctor tried to soothe her or ease her guilt, he was unable to find a cure for her misery.

> Out, damned spot!
> Out I say
> —Lady Macbeth

After days of marching, Malcolm, Macduff, and their newly recruited army of English supporters had arrived in Scotland to fight King Macbeth. They gathered with the other rebel lords who had set up a secret camp near Birnam Woods.

News soon reached Macbeth that trouble was brewing.

"English troops?" Macbeth spat. "Led by Macduff and Malcolm? I'm not afraid of them." The witches had told him that he didn't need to fear Macduff. He trusted them—they had never been wrong before.

Just then, Macbeth's messenger arrived with shocking news: Lady Macbeth had died of grief.

But Macbeth pretended not to hear him. All he could think of was beating Malcolm and Macduff. He was certain that he was invincible.

"I have nothing left to lose," Macbeth said determinedly. "Death doesn't frighten me anymore. Let's see if Birnam Wood really does come to Dunsinane!"

> I will not be afraid of death and bane, till Birnam Forest come to Dunsinane
> —Macbeth

Back in Birnam Woods, Malcolm and Macduff had given orders to their troops.

"Use branches from the trees as camouflage," they said. "Then march to Dunsinane!"

44

From his castle
walls, Macbeth looked
down toward the woods.
Was he going crazy?
The trees were moving,
moving ever closer
toward Dunsinane...

The witches had told
him that he was safe until Birnam Woods
marched toward him. That was exactly
what was happening now! Macbeth had no
choice but to go
into battle.

"Throw down your
branches!" Malcolm
commanded his troops.
"Charge!"

> Make all our
> trumpets speak; give
> them all breath, those
> clamorous harbingers
> of blood and death
> —Malcolm

The battle began, and Macbeth came face to face with his enemies.

"Give up, you coward!" Macduff cried.

"Never," Macbeth sneered.

They fought bitterly, until Macduff finally killed Macbeth.

Before delivering the final blow, Macduff told Macbeth that he had been cut out of his mother's womb in an operation called a caesarean. So Macduff was not born of a woman, just like the witches had foretold. He was the killer that the witches had warned Macbeth about.

Now Macbeth lay dead at Macduff's feet. Macduff chopped off Macbeth's head and walked back to the camp, holding the severed head high.

"Hail, King Malcolm!"
Macduff called out to
his comrades.

"Hail, king of Scotland!"
cheered his fellow soldiers
and bowed to their new king, Malcolm.

"Thank you—all of you," Malcolm said.
"We have seen enough cruelty and hatred
in our land for now. Everyone in exile can
return. Peace should settle. I am honored
to be named your king."

So thanks to all at
once and to each one,
whom we invite to
see us crowned
at Scone
– Malcolm

Out on the heath, the witches
gathered around their cauldron
once again. Dropping a toad
and an adder into their
pot, they stirred their
potion, looking to see
what the future had
in store...

The end

Consultant: Dr. Tamsin Theresa Badcoe
Editor: Alexandra Koken
Designer: Andrew Crowson

Copyright © QEB Publishing 2012

First published in the United States by
QEB Publishing, Inc
3 Wrigley, Suite A
Irvine, CA 92618

www.qed-publishing.co.uk

A CIP record for this book is available from the Library of Congress.

ISBN 978 1 60992 239 9

Printed in China